Voices I

A Short, ʹ

Kali ᴍɪᴄᴋ

6 f, 3 m

Being a teenager is rough, especially when the voice in your head is screaming to get out. *Voices In My Head* follows the story of Evelyn, Gavin, and Emma as they navigate their way through life, love, and learning to speak up.

Characters:

Evelyn Smith. Abi's daughter. Emma's best friend. Anxiety/Depression. (15)

Evelyn II. Voice inside Evelyn's head. (15)

Abi Smith. Evelyn's mom. (41)

Gavin Palmer. Connor's son. Anxiety. (15)

Gavin II. Voice inside Gavin's head. (15)

Connor Palmer. Gavin's dad. (39)

Emma Bernard. Ava's sister. Evelyn's best friend. Anxiety. (16)

Emma II. Voice inside Emma's head. (16)

Ava Bernard. Emma's older sister. (26)

Optional Background Characters (Non-Speaking):

Students. (14-18)
Teachers. (20s+)
People At Funeral. (Any Age.)

Dedicated to Tish, Aurora, Teddy, and my family for keeping me safe and healthy.

To my friends for helping me build this story and my happiness.

To Ms. Christine Vroome, Ms. Lois Holz, and Ms. Leah Bassoff for being so supportive throughout my process of writing this play.

To members of the Broadway community for inspiring me to take chances and follow my dreams.

To anyone who was/is dealing with a mental illness. This book goes out to you, and I send my wishes for a safe road to recovery.

To myself, for gathering the courage to share my story through writing. A dream has finally come true.

"Dreams are illustrations from the book your soul is writing about you." - Marsha Norman

"Love is a serious mental illness."
-Plato

WARNING! This Play Contains The Following Triggers:

- Depression
- Anxiety
- Suicide
- Self-Harm
- Cutting

Stay safe and read this play with caution.

Voices In My Head Script

Act 1

Scene 1

A High School. Mid to late 2010s.

EVELYN is standing center stage. EVELYN II is sitting on a chair directly behind her. A single spotlight is cast on EVELYN as she looks up at the audience.

Evelyn: Lights up on me. I'm Evelyn. I'm average. Pretty happy. Pretty smart. You know. Pretty normal.

EVELYN motions for EVELYN II to come stand by her. The spotlight shifts to EVELYN II.

Evelyn II: Um when's it my turn? I'm Evelyn II, the voice inside her head. I'm a little dark and *(sarcastically)* not at all sarcastic. What my dear, dear friend Evelyn is trying to say is that she's pretty normal. Well, on the outside. On the inside, she's filled with sadness and panic. Oh, and boys.

EVELYN gently flicks EVELYN II'S head; EVELYN II rolls her eyes and takes a step sideways.

Evelyn: You weren't supposed to tell them that!

Evelyn II: I'm usually *screaming* to get out. But I've finally found a chance to speak up.

Evelyn: Lights up.

All the stage lights come on as the scene turns to a school classroom. EVELYN walks to a seat in the back of the room.

Evelyn: We start on a day like any other. The sun shining, the birds screeching, idiots roaming the halls. I take my seat in the back of the classroom.

Lights up on Emma.

The stage turns dark as a single spotlight is cast on the seat next to EVELYN. We see EMMA, a small, shy girl with her nose in a book. Behind her sits EMMA II, the voice inside EMMA'S head. Another spotlight is put on EVELYN.
Evelyn: Emma has been my best friend since kindergarten. We are like family, and I'm so lucky to have someone like her in my life. She is the bes-

Evelyn II: *(Overlapping)* Very annoying. She can't stand up for herself. *(Beat)* Ever.

EVELYN stands up and walks over to the front of EMMA'S desk. EVELYN grabs EMMA'S book out of her hands.

Emma: *(Startled)* Hey Evelyn! How are you?

Emma II: Crap. Did we have homework? Better ask Evelyn, the teacher's pet. *(Rolls eyes)*

Evelyn: I'm doing okay.

EMMA nods and turns towards the classroom door. GAVIN enters the classroom and takes his seat in front of EVELYN.

Emma: Pause.

Lights fade, spotlights on EMMA and EMMA II as they stand up and face the audience.

Emma: *(To audience)* Lights up on Gavin.

Another spotlight lights up GAVIN'S tired face.

Emma: Evelyn's-

Emma II: Not so secret-

Emma: Crush.

EMMA sits back down as the lights come back up. EMMA II stands behind her.

Evelyn: *(Whispers)* Oh my god, Emma. Do you see how cute Gavin looks today?

GAVIN yawns and messes up hair.

Evelyn: *(Pushy)* Go talk to him!

Emma: Okay. Anything for you.

Emma II: It sucks having the same crush as Evelyn. She just asked me to talk to him! What if I mess it up for both of us?

Talking gets quicker.

Emma II: What if I say something embarrassing about me or her? What if he ignores me? What if he doesn't like me? What if-

Evelyn: What are you waiting for?! Go before class starts!

EMMA takes a deep breath and walks over to GAVIN. GAVIN lights up when he sees EMMA.

Gavin II: Oh my god. She just approached you! Don't say something stupid Gavin!

Gavin: Uh hey Emma!

Emma II: He knows my name oh my gosh. *(Fans herself)* Don't say something stupid Emma!

Emma: Hi. Uh-

A school bell sounds. EMMA quickly turns around and walks back to her seat.

Emma II: Thank God. Saved by the bell. I can't embarrass myself at all when I talk to him.

Gavin II: Oh no. She hates me. I messed up. I MESSED UP!

GAVIN takes an eraser and rapidly moves it back and forth on his wrist, harming himself. GAVIN quietly shrieks in pain.
Gavin II: This is what I deserve for being worthless. I keep messing up around her!

Evelyn II: *(To audience)* And with this we begin the tale of the world inside our heads.

Blackout

Scene 2

EVELYN'S home.
A clean living room with a large couch in the middle. The living room connects to a small, tidy kitchen. The front door opens to the living room.
EVELYN II sits on the couch next to EVELYN, loudly eating.

Evelyn: Can you stop? Like now?

Evelyn II: Why should I? Just working up our mind to make it stressed out about tonight's massive homework load!

EVELYN rolls her eyes.

Evelyn: Well isn't that a wonderful thing to think about! Especially after this horrible day. I can't believe I didn't get to talk to Gavin once!

Evelyn II: *(Spacy)* Yes, academics are a very wonderful thing to think about.

Evelyn: Snap out of it! We have bigger problems than writing that essay. I gotta figure out how to win over Gavin, since Emma seemed to have messed things up.

EVELYN reaches into her backpack and grabs a torn apart red notebook. The cover reads "101 Ways to Get a Boy to Like You."

Evelyn II: Ah, yes. Smart choice. One hundred and one ways to get a boy to like you, by Evelyn Smith and Emma Bernard. 4th grade. *(Sarcastically)* What a year that was. Why do I always carry it around with me?

EVELYN carefully brings the red notebook up to her face and blows dust off the cover. EVELYN sneezes and laughs. EVELYN flips through a few pages before landing on page 25.

Evelyn: Way number twenty-five: do NOT have a friend approach the lucky guy. (Beat) Well, already broke that rule.

EVELYN takes out a pencil case from her backpack and grabs a large red marker. EVELYN crosses out the title on this page and sighs. EVELYN sets the book down and sinks down into the couch.

Evelyn: Man. Emma and Gavin were only standing a few feet away from me.
Evelyn II: Why was I pretending not to notice them? Why didn't I listen to make sure she was talking about me? Saying nice things about me?

Evelyn: She's the only person that knows about my love for him.

Evelyn II: She said something. I know it. He never liked me. He never will. Thanks a lot, Emma!

EVELYN'S breathing gets heavier.

Evelyn II: What'd I do to deserve this? My own best friend betraying me? Dammit Emma. I thought I could trust you.

Evelyn: But what if she did say nice things?

Evelyn II: *(on the verge of tears)* No, she wouldn't. I hate myself. I hate this. Why live if I can't find love?

EVELYN, followed by EVELYN II, tip toes over to the kitchen. EVELYN looks around, before finally locating a box of sharp knives.

Evelyn: This'll do it. Take away some of the hatred I have for myself, and Emma, and even Gavin.

EVELYN carefully opens the box and grabs a sharp knife and holds it up to the light. EVELYN raises the blade and slowly brings it down to her skin. Before being able to cut herself, EVELYN hears a knock at the door, causing her to quickly scramble to put the knife back in the box. Evelyn's mom ABI enters.

Abi: I'm home! Evelyn, where are you?

ABI closes and locks the door behind her. ABI walks past the couch and notices the red notebook. ABI picks it up and studies it for a moment.

Abi: Evelyn, come here. What is this?

EVELYN hurries from the kitchen into the living room.

Evelyn: Oh, nothing. Just a book for school, because we both know how important that is!

Evelyn II: Shoot! I forgot to put it away. Oh no. Oh no. If my mom finds out, she'll think I wasn't focusing on school. Oh no. Goodbye, sweet book.

Abi: Well are you taking a class on how to flirt with boys?

EVELYN looks down and shakes her head no.
Abi: That's what I thought. Come on Evelyn. Why can't you ever focus on school? You're failing! You only got an A- on your last project in social studies. Do you know how that makes me feel? I feel like I failed as a mother. I taught you right. I taught you how to do this, do that correctly. I tried to set you up for a good life. I really did. But you're failing. You can only focus on school.

Evelyn II: *(Shouting over Abi)* SHUT UP. SHUT UP. SHUT UP. It was an A-. That was the best grade out of anyone in the class. God, I wish she'd just listen to me. I wish she supported me and cared about ME. Not school. Not grades. Just me.

Abi: Got it?

EVELYN shakes her head yes and looks up from the ground. ABI looks around the living room and locates a small box. ABI opens it and pulls out a lighter.

Abi: Would you like to do the honors?

EVELYN shakes her head and dashes off stage. ABI rips out a page of the book and lights it on fire and exits through the kitchen.

Blackout

Scene 3

EMMA and her sister's apartment.
There's trash and clothes everywhere. In the middle of the room is one large bed. AVA sits on the bed writing in a journal. EMMA walks in the door, followed by EMMA II.

Ava: Hey! Look who's back!

AVA sets her journal down and gives EMMA a big hug. EMMA immediately pushes her away.

Ava: No hug? Even from me? Wow. Today must've been really bad. Come sit next to therapist Ava.

EMMA lets out a giggle and sits next to AVA. EMMA II sits behind the pair.

Ava: Okay. Speak to me.

Emma: So, you know Gavin, right? The cute brown-haired dork who sits in front of me?

Ava: Well of course I do. You talk about him non-stop. In fact, I think I know a little *too* much about him.

EMMA blushes and turns away.

Ava: Okay, okay. Sorry. Tell Ava what happened.

Emma II: Why does she always get up in all my business? Yeah, she's my sister and legal guardian, well ever since mom and dad died. But still. IT ISN'T HER JOB!

Emma: You know my best friend Evelyn, right?

AVA nods.

Ava: How could I not know Evelyn!

Emma: Well, today during first period she asked me to go talk to Gavin for her. Did I tell you Evelyn also has a huge crush on him? She can get super annoying about it. She's always obsessing over him-

Emma II: Like a complete stalker!

Emma: -to the point where she can't even be in the same room as him without risking making a fool out of herself.

AVA lets out a little laugh. EMMA rolls her eyes.

Emma: Anyways, she doesn't know I like him. Knowing Evelyn, if I even mentioned his name to her she'd think I'm a backstabber. When I'm not! When she asked me to talk to Gavin, I was excited. I don't think we've really ever talked. Yet somehow, he knew my name! All I managed to say was "Hi" before the bell rang and I turned around and walked back to my desk. And then uh- *(Beat)* never mind.

Ava: Tell me! Come on, silly girl.

Emma II: Silly girl? Really? Does she understand how much she is hurting me by saying that. God, Ava really doesn't know me at all. She doesn't bother to think of me as anything else except some silly, happy girl! Does she think I <u>wanted</u> to live with her after mom and dad died in that awful car crash? NO! I would definitely rather live with Evelyn and her crazy mother. Their death hurt me. It hurt a lot, and it still hurts. Being a "silly girl" is the exact opposite of how I feel. If she's gonna see who I really am behind my smile, I'm gonna have to confess about what I saw.

Emma: Okay, I'll tell you. As the bell rang, I turned around to look at him one last time. But I saw him angrily running an eraser across his wrist. I saw blood begin to leak from the wound. What does it mean? What do I do?

EMMA is on the verge of tears.

Emma: What if I caused this? I can't bear to think of that. *(Now crying)* W-w-what do I d-do?

AVA gives EMMA a giant bear hug.

Ava: Emma! I'm so sorry you had to see that. I don't know what to do. *(Tense)* I really don't. Maybe talk to him about it. Maybe sit in a quiet place and talk. Be his friend. Try to help. I wish I knew what to do. I really do wish.

EMMA squeezes AVA even tighter. They sit in silence for a moment.

Ava: Hey Emma?

Emma II: Uh oh.

Emma: Yeah?

Ava: If you ever think about harming yourself, even the slightest bit, please tell me.

EMMA lets go of AVA and nods. EMMA lays her head in AVA'S lap. AVA strokes EMMA'S hair.

Ava: It's all going to be alright. I promise. It's all going to be alright.

Blackout

Scene 4

GAVIN'S home.
In the middle of a nice, tidy room, GAVIN sits on a large couch.
There's a vase of flowers with a single large lily in the middle
sitting on a small table next to the couch. GAVIN writes in a
journal while GAVIN II reads what he is writing.

Gavin II: September 3rd. Math class was rough today. Mr. Johnson was all x-squared this, negative that. It's so confusing! Why don't numbers click in my head the same way they do in Emma's?

GAVIN sighs and smiles at the thought of EMMA.

GAVIN II: Oh Emma. I can't stop thinking about our interaction earlier today. She said one word to me before the bell rang! Why does school have to ruin everything? I was finally getting a chance to talk to the most beautiful girl in the world! Except her best friend is kinda weird. I think her name is Evelyn. She is always staring at me with some awkward look on her face. I don't know why. Kinda creepy.

The front door unlocks, and CONNOR enters the living room with a phone pressed against his ear. GAVIN quickly hides the journal underneath a couch cushion.

Gavin: Dad! You're home! Can I ask you for some adv-

Connor: *(Into the phone)* Give me just a second guys, my son is acting up again. Gotta love teenagers!

CONNOR looks over at GAVIN and motions to his phone.

Connor: Not now!

CONNOR quickly walks off stage, phone still up against his ear. After he exits, GAVIN looks around to make sure CONNOR is gone before grabbing the journal from under the cushion.

Gavin II: Why did I get stuck with this guy as my dad! He constantly ignores me. I don't really think he knows I exist. He's always on the phone or in his office working. Ever since mom left us last year, he hasn't paid attention to anything but work! I could really use his help right now. My first big crush! How do I get her to like me? How do I impress her? What do I do?

GAVIN pulls his phone from out of his pocket.
Gavin: Google search. How to get a girl to like you. Aha! Here's a good article. Three easy steps to impress your crush. Step one. Buy her flowers and ask her somewhere. I know! Our fall formal is coming up next weekend. Maybe I should ask her. But what to do about the flowers...

GAVIN looks around the room until he spots the vase of flowers.

Gavin: Perfect! This beautiful lily right here in the middle will do.

GAVIN takes the lily from the vase and holds it to his chest.

Gavin: Mission get the girl has officially started.

Gavin II: But what if she doesn't say yes? What if she completely rejects me? What if the flower dies? So much can go wrong! What if-

Gavin: *(Loudly)* UGH.

Connor: *(From offstage)* SHUT UP!

GAVIN leans back on the couch and takes a deep breath before sniffing the lily and closing his eyes.

Blackout

Scene 5

A High School.

GAVIN is sitting at a desk in the middle of the room, flipping through a math textbook.
EMMA enters the classroom and takes a seat behind GAVIN.

Emma II: Thank god Evelyn isn't here right now. The doctor's office really does save lives, like mine right now. With Evelyn away, I can maybe get a chance to talk to Gavin!

EMMA glances at the watch on her wrist.

Emma II: I still have 7 minutes before school starts. Right now is the perfect time to ask about what I saw.

Gavin II: Oh my gosh. She's sitting right behind me. She's right there. What do I say? What do I do? Someone help me!

GAVIN grabs his pencil from his backpack and examines the eraser. GAVIN sets the pencil on his wrist.

Emma: *(Concerned)* Gavin stop!

GAVIN looks over at her, shocked.

Gavin II: Oh no. Did she just see me get ready to harm myself? What does she think it was? Does she think I'm crazy?

Emma II: It's go time, Emma.

EMMA takes a deep breath.

Emma: Hey Gavin, can I talk to you in the hall? Alone?

GAVIN blushes and nods.

Gavin: I've been meaning to speak to you alone too.

GAVIN and EMMA exit the classroom, standing in front of a wall of lockers.

Gavin II: Now's your time to make a move!

GAVIN pulls out the lily sticking out of his back pants pocket and holds it behind his back.

Emma: So, who wants to go first?

Both awkwardly laugh.

Gavin: I guess I will.

Gavin II: Come on Gavin, have courage! Make that move!

GAVIN takes a huge breath and loudly exhales.

Gavin: Emma Bernard, will you- um.

Emma: Will I what?

Gavin: *(All in one breath.)* Emma, will you go to the dance with me?

Emma II: OHMYGOD. YES.

Emma: Emma, who? Me, Emma? Emma, me?

GAVIN nods his head and holds the lily out to her.

Gavin: Um. Yes, you Emma. I've been wanting to ask you that for a long time. Oh, this is for you.

EMMA takes the flower and sniffs it. EMMA smiles and places it in her hair.

Gavin: So, um. *Will* you go to the dance with me?

Emma: I've also got something I've wanted to say for a long time: YES!

GAVIN and EMMA embrace as EVELYN walks down the hall. EVELYN is carrying her stuff that she needs for class. When EVELYN sees GAVIN and EMMA embrace, she is shocked. EVELYN drops her stack of heavy books, creating a loud sound. The sound startles EMMA and GAVIN, who turn around and see EVELYN standing there.

Evelyn II: *(Angry)* What the hell did I just witness?!

EVELYN II turns to the audience.

Evelyn II: Lights DOWN.

The stage goes dark as the scene freezes. A single spotlight is cast on EVELYN II. EVELYN II paces around, angry and hurt.

Evelyn II: What did I just witness? Did they just hug? Did they REALLY JUST HUG? I poured my heart out to Emma about everything. About love, about Gavin. She watched, and encouraged me to obsess over him. She liked watching me write "Evelyn and Gavin Forever" and "Future Evelyn Palmer" in all my notebooks. I should've noticed! This was to cover up her own secret obsession with him! I can't believe she did this to me. Just because I went to a doctor's appointment doesn't mean it's okay to go and steal the man who was supposed to end up with me! I now have no friends, no crush. Why live if your life has no meaning?

EVELYN II stops pacing and takes a breath.

Evelyn II: *(Through gritted teeth)* Lights up.

The scene resumes as the lights slowly fade back up.

Evelyn: Well, well, well. What do we have here? Do either of you lovebirds want to explain what's going on? How about Emma!

Come on Emma, my old pal. My forever buddy. Want to tell me, your best friend, what's happening?
EMMA stares at her shoes.

Emma II: Oh no. Oh no. I just got my chance with the man who I was supposed to end up with. But, I probably just lost my friend. Not just my friend, but my BEST friend! We've known each other for 13 years. It can't end like this. We can't end like this. E squared, best friends forever and always, can't end like this.

Emma: *(Struggling to find words)* Evelyn! I, uh, I can explain!

Evelyn: Oh, I'm sure you can! What's with the lily in your hair? The nice embrace? Surely something is going on.

GAVIN and EMMA keep staring at the floor as EVELYN looks them up and down.

Evelyn: Since Emma is no help, let's try you Gavin! Sweet, sweet Gavin. Would YOU like to tell me what's going on?

Gavin II: I knew she was weird. I knew Evelyn was creepy. Keep cool, calm and courageous

Gavin: I asked Emma to the fall formal with me this weekend.

Evelyn: Oh, how wonderful! And Emma, what was your answer.

EMMA says nothing and continues to look down.

Gavin: To my liking, she said yes. She took this beautiful lily as a pledge. We embraced out of the gratitude we have for one another. Why is that a problem? More importantly, why is that YOUR problem?

Evelyn: Wow, thank you for that very detailed explanation! Would you mind if I stole Emma for a second to talk to her? Privately?

Gavin: Anything you say to her, you can say to me.

Evelyn: Well alrighty then! The two people in love stay together! Was it really this meant to be? Find out next time on "Emma betrays her best friend!" Get the hell out of here Gavin. Go! Now! Faster!

EVELYN stomps her foot and points to the door of the classroom. GAVIN quickly scurries inside.

EVELYN walks around EMMA a few times, before standing directly in front of EMMA. EVELYN looks up and down at EMMA before shaking her head.

Evelyn: You backstabbing bitch.

EVELYN violently slaps EMMA on the cheek. EMMA loudly screams out and falls to the floor, causing GAVIN to rush outside the classroom. EVELYN angrily storms away as GAVIN holds EMMA in his arms. They stare at each other, breathing heavily.

Blackout

Scene 6

Entire cast except for EMMA II and GAVIN II stands in a line at the front of the stage. EVELYN stands in the middle, in between EVELYN II and ABI. Next to ABI stands GAVIN and CONNOR. Next to EVELYN II stands EMMA and AVA.

Evelyn II: The world inside our heads is a dark, crazy place. Maybe-

Evelyn: If I took a deep breath and asked about others once in a while,

Abi: If I looked a little deeper into someone's life,

Connor: If I balanced my heavy rocks into a sculpture,

Ava: If I asked more questions and reached out to those I love instead of pretending that everything's fine,

Emma: If I learned to speak my truths,

Gavin: If I learned to believe in myself more,

Evelyn II: We could calm our screaming and shouting and say what we need to say. Maybe this is the beginning of our story, and the secret to writing page one in the book of

ALL: life, love, and happiness.

Entire cast moves closer together and holds hands.

Lights slowly fade away.

<u>End of Act 1.</u>

Act 2

Scene 1

EVELYN is standing center stage. EVELYN II is standing next to her. Two spotlights are cast on EVELYN and EVELYN II as they address the audience.

Evelyn II: The second page of our crazy book of life, love and happiness starts right now.

Evelyn: It's been a month since the incident with Emma.

EMMA quickly enters and stands next to EVELYN.

Emma, Evelyn: We're no longer friends.

Emma: No one knows about what happened in that hallway except, Gavin, Evelyn, and I. It's our own little secret.

Evelyn: The dance came and went.

GAVIN runs onstage and twirls EMMA around. EMMA giggles and smiles.

Gavin: Emma and I have been happily dating for a month now! Oh, and I've stopped the self-harm! I've never been this happy.

GAVIN dips EMMA and they laugh. They hold hands and run offstage. The scene changes into a school classroom.

Evelyn: We once again start with a day like any other.

Evelyn II: At this time, no one knew how much this day would be different. How this day would change lives.

EVELYN sits down at a desk in the back of the classroom. GAVIN and EMMA walk through the door, together, and take seats at the front of the room.

Emma: *(To Gavin)* Do you really think I should do it? Should I really talk to her?

Gavin: Yes, I do. I think it's the best thing for both of you.

Emma II: I really don't want to do this. She always seems so mad at me! Well I can't blame her...

Gavin: Come on Emma! *(Mimicking Shia LaBeouf)* Just do it! EMMA nods and giggles. EMMA takes a deep breath, turns around, and starts to walk towards EVELYN.*

Evelyn II: Why is she walking towards me?

Emma: Um. Hi Evelyn.

Evelyn: What do you want? Are you here to stab me in the back again?

Emma: I'm just here to apologize, okay! I just want to apologize!

Evelyn: Well I don't accept your apology! I trusted you for years. I don't want to be around someone I can't trust. Get away from me and out of my life!

Emma: Fine! I will! I'm MUCH happier without you.

EMMA storms off.

Evelyn II: I can't believe that just happened. Why'd I say that!

Emma II: Why did I just say that!

EMMA sits down next to GAVIN.

Gavin: Well, how'd it go?

Emma: Let's... let's just not talk about it. I should've gotten rid of her a long time ago. She was rude and weird and-

Gavin: Hey, hey! Calm down. It's all gonna be okay.

EMMA lays her head on GAVIN'S shoulder and closes her eyes. From across the room, EVELYN rolls her eyes and loudly coughs, interrupting GAVIN and EMMA'S moment. GAVIN and

EMMA turn around and stare at EVELYN for a few seconds before turning back around. EMMA once again lays her head on GAVIN'S shoulder.

Evelyn II: I wish they would just STOP! I wish it <u>all</u> would just stop! Can't Emma see how much she's hurt me?

EVELYN leans back into her chair and closes her eyes.

Lights Slowly Fade Out

Scene 2

EVELYN'S home.
A clean living room with a large couch in the middle. The living room connects to a small, tidy kitchen. The front door opens to the living room.
EVELYN II sits on the couch next to EVELYN. Both have their eyes closed. There is now a bouquet of lilies on a small table next to the couch.

Evelyn II: Why'd I say that to Emma? I really miss her. But she hurt me! She, she, she lost my trust! I don't have a best friend anymore. I have no one to rely on. I don't know who I am! I have no friends. No one I love. My mom is CRAZY and doesn't care about me. It's all about school this, school that. Emma stole Gavin. She took my dignity with it. I don't know what to do! I feel so worthless. I see that there's no point in doing anything anymore.

ABI noisily opens the front door.

Abi: Evelyn, I'm home!

EVELYN'S eyes suddenly open.

Evelyn: Oh, hi mother.

Abi: What homework have we got today? Let me see your planner. No wait. Let's check your grades first and decide your punishment.

EVELYN shudders and hands her mom her planner.

Abi: Math homework? Questions 1-20 on pages 47-49?

EVELYN pulls out her math notebook and shows the questions to ABI. ABI nods and looks back at the planner.

Abi: English essay on discrimination in the workplace?

EVELYN pulls out her composition notebook and let's ABI read over it.

Abi: That's all you had for tonight. I better see good grades from that tomorrow. Now. Let me see this week's grade sheet.

EVELYN slowly pulls out a sheet from a binder and shakily hands it to her mom.

Evelyn II: Uh oh. I got a B on my math test this week. I was so distracted with Emma and Gavin and my depression that I forgot all about studying for the test. This punishment is going to be bad. I don't know what it'll be, but it's going to be very, very bad.

Abi: A in English, A in social studies, A in science.

ABI'S eye begins to twitch as her face grows tense.

Abi: B in math.

ABI'S hand starts to shake as she crumples up the sheet.

Abi: *(Angry)* WHAT DID YOU DO? HOW COULD YOU DISOBEY ME LIKE THIS? Look me right in the eyes young lady. Who taught you it was OKAY to fail? Who taught you to get a damn B in a class? A B! What were you doing? Why did this happen? What could be more important than school?

Evelyn II: *(Shouting over Abi)* Shut up. Just shut up. Please just stop. JUST STOP. I CAN'T TAKE IT ANYMORE. PLEASE MOTHER. I TRY SO HARD. JUST STOP.

EVELYN II extends her arms out sideways. There is a blackout and the scene stops. A spotlight is cast on EVELYN, who is standing next to EVELYN II. EVELYN takes a deep breath and paces. EVELYN pauses at the table next to the couch and takes a big sniff of the bouquet of lilies.

Evelyn II: A bouquet full of lilies. My favorite flower. Simple and sweet. The smell calms me down and sends me into a safe place in my mind, I feel safe in this own little world. I'm <u>done</u> with everything and everyone. My mother pays no attention to the real me. Gavin loves Emma. Emma loves Gavin. Emma hates me. I have no point in living. I feel it. It's time to go.

EVELYN II extends her arms above her head. The lights come up and the scene resumes.

Abi: What could be more important than pleasing your mother?

EVELYN stares directly into ABI'S eyes.

Evelyn: Nothing.

Evelyn II: Everything.

Evelyn: I'm very sorry, mother.

Abi: You better be. Next time this happens I will take away everything you care about. Everything you love.
Evelyn II: What an easy punishment. I have nothing that I care about and love!

Abi: Do you understand?

Evelyn: Yes. I'm very sorry.

ABI walks offstage while EVELYN sinks into the couch. EVELYN closes her eyes.

Blackout

Scene 3

EMMA and her AVA'S apartment.
There's trash and clothes everywhere. In the middle of the room
is one large bed. AVA lays on the bed, her eyes closed.
EMMA, followed by EMMA II, enters the room.

Ava: *(Startled)* Hey! You're here pretty late! I was getting worried.

Emma: Yep. School bus took a wrong turn on the way back.

AVA and EMMA let out a faint laugh. There's a few moments of awkward silence.

Emma: I think I'll just go do my homework, if that's alright with you.

Ava: Oh, yeah, sure. Go ahead. If you need my help, I'm right here. Get good grades, you happy girl!

EMMA exits the main room into a smaller space with a desk, a chair, and a lamp. EMMA turns the lamp on.

Emma: I can't believe I said what I said to Evelyn today. She didn't deserve it! Truth is, I'm unhappy that I don't have her. I need Evelyn in my life. I love Gavin, but I'm so unhappy! I hide behind my smile every day. Ava thinks I'm fine, Gavin does too. I don't know who to trust, what to say. UGH. I need to make up with Evelyn. But how?

EMMA lays her head on the desk for a moment before springing out of the chair. EMMA digs through her backpack before removing a pencil and sheet of lined paper. EMMA places both things on the desk, and slowly picks the pencil up and starts writing.

Emma II: Dear Evelyn. I am sorry for everything I've said and done in this past month. I know what I said yesterday was not right. Want to know the truth? Well, I really do need you in my life. You were my other half. Gavin can only fill up some of that space. I need you to help make me feel whole again. Oh, and about Gavin. He really isn't that great of a boyfriend. Sure, he's cute and dorky, but we don't do much. I know stealing him from you was a horrible thing for me to do as a friend, but consider yourself lucky. I'm surprised I put up with him for this long. I really hope you'll learn to accept me as a friend again. I would like to have you back in my life. Your friend, no.

EMMA scribbles the words out as EMMA II recites them.

Emma II: Your best friend, no!

EMMA once again scribbles the words out.

Emma II: Your sister, Emma.

EMMA folds the letter and sticks it in her backpack.

Emma: There. I really hope this will at least help her talk to me. We haven't had a decent conversation in over a month! Maybe I should ask Ava on how to approach her. Ava will know what to do.

EMMA exits the study and sits next to AVA on the bed.

Ava: What brings you here?

Emma: Have you ever lost a friend, then tried to become friends with them again?

Ava: Yes. All the time. Why?

Emma: Oh. It's about Evelyn.

Ava: Ah, I see. Why do you want to be her friend again?

Emma: Because without her, I feel like a part of me is missing. We were friends for thirteen years. Thirteen whole years! It's been so hard for me to function knowing that she's mad at me. Help!

Ava: Woah, calm down there buddy. Let's see. I'd say to start with a note, telling her how you feel about your friendship.

Emma: Done. I'm gonna give her my note tomorrow.

Ava: Typical Emma, always one step ahead of me.

AVA rolls her eyes as EMMA laughs.

Emma: Well? What's next?!

Ava: Hmm. Let me think. *(Beat)* Well first I think you need to see how she responds to the letter. If it's positive, then try to start a conversation. If you see her in the hall, ask her about what class she has next or what she ate for dinner last night. Keep it simple. That's the first few steps. If all goes as planned and she responds positively, then come to me for the next step. Got it?

Emma: Got it! Thank you, Ava, you're the best sister ever!
Ava: No problem.

EMMA gives AVA a big hug.

Lights fade Out

Scene 4

GAVIN'S home.
In the middle of a nice, tidy room, GAVIN sits on a large couch.
GAVIN is writing in a journal with a pencil.

Gavin II: November 12th. I found out I got an A on my English essay today! My dad would be so proud. But he probably will never know. He's always talking on his damn phone. It's like I don't exist. I'm a piece of dust that he keeps flicking off his shoulder. He's the reason I used to harm myself. He made me feel like I was worthless. He made me feel as if I didn't matter. Now that Emma's in my life, I feel so much joy. I feel things that I've never felt before. I feel, I feel. I feel loved. I feel appreciated. And I try to give her all those things in return. If only my dad would-

The front door unlocks and CONNOR walks in, phone on his ear. GAVIN quickly hides the journal under a couch cushion.

Connor: *(Into phone)* Yep. Got it, Uh huh. See you.

CONNOR hangs up the phone. GAVIN stares at him.

Connor: What're you looking at? Come give your old man a hug!

GAVIN hesitates, then walks over and gives CONNOR a small, quick hug.

Connor: Come on, I know you can do better than that!

GAVIN rolls his eyes and squeezes CONNOR tight.

Connor: There we go.

CONNOR sits on the couch and motions for GAVIN to sit too. GAVIN sits on the couch next to CONNOR.

Connor: Okay son. Tell me about your life.

GAVIN'S face lights up.

Gavin: Well, I got an A on my English essay!

Connor: Good job! What else?

Gavin: So, there's this girl. Her name is-

CONNOR'S phone starts to ring again. CONNOR mouths 'Sorry' to GAVIN and rushes off the stage, phone pressed to his ear. GAVIN rolls his eyes and sinks deeper into the couch.

Gavin II: God I wish he would spend some time with me. He knows nothing about me! Does he know my favorite color? It's blue. My favorite food? Chocolate cake. Who's Emma? Why, she's the sweetest, smartest, most amazing person ever. She's the opposite of Dad. I hate him. Who's he talking to anyways! He always says its work but why does he have to be on calls all the time? It's just not right! I know nothing about him! What's his favorite color? Favorite food? I may never know! Soon I'll be off to college. Dad won't even notice I'm gone. I don't know who my dad is, even though he's been 10 feet and a cellphone away from me all this time.

GAVIN pulls the journal back out from under the couch cushion.

Gavin: At least I'll always have my trusty journal. My journal actually listens and accepts me. Where was I?

GAVIN resumes writing.

Gavin II: If only my dad would listen. I feel like I write that sentence every day, waiting for something to happen about it. Only time will tell, I guess. It's not like I can tell my dad to get off his phone! Okay, enough about dad. I need to talk about Emma's interaction with what's her name? Emily? Oh! Right. It's Evelyn. Don't like her. I need to know what Emma said to Evelyn, and what Evelyn said that made Emma so upset! She seemed sad all day and was moping around. This was very unlike her. All I could hear was yelling from the back of the classroom. I was terrified. I always knew Evelyn was a little weird, a little off. I just, I just hope Emma's alright. I know how much she really wanted to make up with Evelyn. Apparently, they were friends for 13 years. 13 years! How cold poor Emma put up with Evelyn's, uh,

GAVIN makes air quotes.

Gavin II: "Weirdness." I just hope Emma, and even Evelyn are alright. I hate seeing people sad. I wish there was something I could do! It was all my fault they were fighting! Why is everything bad all my fault? I did this! It would all be fine if I didn't get involved!

GAVIN stops writing and looks at his pencil. GAVIN sniffs the eraser and nods. GAVIN dramatically raises the pencil up, eraser side down, and swipes it across his arm. GAVIN does this several times, until blood starts flowing down his wrist. GAVIN keeps swiping and screams out in pain.

Connor: *(From offstage)* GAVIN! SHUT UP! I'M ON A CALL!

GAVIN throws the pencil to the floor and grabs his arm. He falls off the couch, weeping.

Blackout

Scene 5

EVELYN'S room.
There's one large bed in the middle of the room. There are
multiple shelves on the walls. The shelves are full of trinkets. On
one shelf is a box of sleeping pills.
EVELYN and EVELYN II are sitting on the bed. EVELYN is
writing on a piece of paper. After reading over it, EVELYN folds
the paper and places it in her pocket.

Evelyn II: Why does she always have to be so cruel? Why does she always have to be so cruel TO ME? I've never done anything to her! I study hard, I cooperate, what more could she want?

EVELYN loudly screams into a pillow.

Abi: *(From offstage)* No noise while you're grounded! Next sound means something is getting taken away.

EVELYN rolled her eyes, shuddered, and plopped back onto the bed.

Evelyn II: WHY! I can't go on like this anymore. I really can't. I'm done.

EVELYN and EVELYN II begin to pace around the room.

Evelyn II: I think it's really time to do this. I mean, I've waited so long so why not do it now, when it'll really hurt. I've been so good to Emma! What did I do to deserve this? I've supported her for, well, for forever! What else could I do? I've told her all my secrets, all my... everything! She knew I liked him. Oh Gavin. I wish I could see your reaction when you find out what happened to me. I've never had any friends except Emma, the pressures on me all the time at home. One mistake around my mom and it will set her off. You know what? I've never heard her praise me. Not once. No compliments, no thank you. It always feels like I'm doing stuff for her. I mean, she's always complaining about me so won't her life be easier if I just go away?

EVELYN and EVELYN II'S pacing gets faster and faster with each word. EVELYN breaks into a cold sweat.

But for forever. Maybe that'll show her to care about me. I've always been a good student. I've always been privileged. But with a mother who doesn't care about me unless I make a mistake, and even then it's putting me down. I try so hard. I've always tried so hard. I've attempted this before, but I think it's really time to go.

EVELYN notices the box of sleeping pills on a shelf. She grabs the box, examines it, and opens it up, revealing a bottle of pills. EVELYN opens it, pops one in her mouth, and swallows it.

Evelyn II: Goodbye Emma, my backstabbing best friend. Goodbye mother, you ignorant, obsessed woman. Goodbye Gavin, my one true love. Goodbye cruel world. I hope, *(Beat)* no wait. I know you'll be better without me.

Evelyn: *(Raising the pill bottle to her mouth, ready to swallow multiple)* Lights out.

Blackout

In the dark we hear a loud noise, signaling that EVELYN has fallen to the floor. The lights suddenly brightly flash up at the audience, blinding them for a moment.

Scene 6

EVELYN'S room.
A while later, ABI knocks on EVELYN'S door. When EVELYN doesn't answer, ABI bursts into EVELYN'S room. Inside EVELYN'S room, EVELYN is lying on her back with a mostly empty bottle of sleeping pills next to her. There are pills scattered everywhere on the floor, especially by EVELYN'S head. EVELYN II stands right next to EVELYN'S dead body. There is a small folded up note sticking out of EVELYN'S pocket.

When she sees this, ABI lets out a loud, chilling shriek.

Abi: EVELYN! EVELYN WAKE UP!

ABI frantically pushes, pulls, and pokes EVELYN'S body in an attempt to revive it. This motion goes on for quite some time, before ABI comes to the realization that EVELYN is dead. ABI kneels and sinks into her knees. ABI keeps loudly crying out for help. When no one answers, ABI aggressively wraps her arms around EVELYN'S body and lays her head on EVELYN'S stomach. EVELYN II mournfully watches ABI weep.

Evelyn II: Wow. She finally cares about me. Me! She can't worry about school. She can't worry about my grades. It's finally my turn. It sickens me that I had to die to do it. Death reveals someone's true colors, what they really care about. I wonder how Emma and Gavin will react. I hope it hits them hard. It's what they deserve.

ABI finishes crying and kisses EVELYN on the cheek before walking out of EVELYN'S room, making sure to turn off the light as she walks out. After ABI exits, she quickly returns to the room and turns the light on. ABI looks around, grabs the folded note out of EVELYN'S pocket, and walks out, once again turning off the lights.

Blackout

Scene 7

A High School.
EMMA is standing by her locker in the hallway. EMMA is
rummaging through her backpack, trying to find her note to
EVELYN.

Emma II: Where is that note! That's the only way I'm ever going to be Evelyn's friend again. I NEED that note. Okay, where was it? Not in this pocket, not in the back pocket. Not in my lunchbox, where could it be?

EMMA unzips the very front pocket of her backpack.

Emma: Aha! Got it! I really hope this works. I'm not the same without Evelyn.

EMMA walks towards the classroom door. GAVIN quickly comes running down the hallway, his eyes red from crying. GAVIN embraces EMMA from behind.

Emma: Well that was weird. Are you just trying to give me encouragement to make up with Evelyn today? I wrote her a note. I hope it works! Thanks for supporting me!

Gavin: Oh. You don't know, then.

Emma II: What is going on?

Emma: What don't I know?

Gavin: I'm so sorry.

Emma II: Okay, something weird is going on.

EMMA II starts to pace as her talking gets faster.

Emma II: Why was Gavin crying? Is he alright? Did I do something? Is he breaking up with me? Is it about Ava? What happened to Ava! Oh no! What's going on?

EMMA II takes a deep breath,

Emma II: Come on, Emma. Be strong. I'm sure it couldn't be that bad.

Emma: Gavin. Tell me what's going on.

Gavin II: What do I say! I can't do this. But how else will she find out! Probably by someone she doesn't trust. That means she needs to hear it from me. Come on, Gavin, Be strong.

GAVIN loudly inhales and exhales. GAVIN grabs both of EMMA'S hands.

Gavin: Emma. It's about Evelyn.

EMMA'S eyes grow wide.

Gavin: She-she's…

GAVIN bursts into tears and starts yelling.

Gavin: She's gone! Evelyn is gone. She's, she's gone! Forever. She-she…

GAVIN drops to the floor. A teary-eyed, frightened EMMA kneels down and grabs GAVIN'S hands.

Emma II: No. This can't be happening.

Emma: Gavin. What happened.

Gavin: *(All in one breath)* Evelyn committed suicide by overdosing on sleeping pills.

Emma II: No. This didn't happen. She's alive. She's still here, she's still my best friend!
EMMA stands up and takes off running down the hall. She runs outside the school and sits on a bench. EMMA is weeping, her head in her hands. After a few moments of this, ABI comes and sits by EMMA.

Emma: Tell me it isn't true.

Abi: Then I won't speak.

EMMA loudly sobs. ABI puts her arms around EMMA and squeezes her tight.

Abi: She wanted you to have this.

ABI pulls out the folded piece of paper EVELYN wrote.

Abi: She didn't leave any other notes for anyone else. Just you. *(Beat)* Go on, open it.

EMMA slowly opens the note and reads it.

Emma II: Dear Emma, if you're reading this right now that means I'm dead. I've escaped a world that I did not feel welcome in. I am leaving everything to you. Take care of my mom. She may have hated me, but she still is a person. Take care of yourself. Take care of Gavin. Know that I am much happier where I am now. I will forever be with you. I'll be there in your hearts. I wish we could've made up. I think we both know that no matter how hard we tried, it wasn't an option. Tell everyone I'm okay, I'm better. Tell everyone I love them. I'm sending you lilies to use at the funeral I am asking you to plan. Stay safe Emma. Do the right thing. Use the little voice that's inside your head to speak up. Love, Evelyn.

EMMA wipes a tear from her face and sniffles.

Abi: Can I read it?

Emma: *(Stern. Almost Yelling)* No. No matter how much you want to, no. Her life is in my hands from now on. I need to fix something. Stay safe, Ms. Smith. Expect an invitation to her funeral in your mailbox soon.

ABI stares at EMMA, hurt.

Emma: *(Tearfully)* I-I-I. I'm sorry.

EMMA runs back inside the school. ABI slowly gets up and leaves.

Blackout

Scene 8

A funeral home.

The tone is dark and sad. There's a big casket at center stage. Pictures of EVELYN and vases of lilies fill the room. Full cast is in black and sitting on benches, waiting for EMMA to speak. ABI stands at a microphone.

Abi: Please welcome Evelyn's best friend Emma Bernard to speak about the memories she had with my little girl.

EMMA slowly walks to the microphone.

Emma: Friends and family. Today we gather to mourn the death of Evelyn Christine Smith. Evelyn was exceptional. She was insanely smart. Always was at the top of her class. Took AP and honors classes every year. I don't know how she did it, but she somehow managed to complete her homework every night. I know Abi would be pleased to hear this. Evelyn achieved grades higher than 90% of the class. She would tell me about all the pressure you put on her, Abi. I want you to take her death as a time to start over and look deeper into someone's life. Don't look at them as a puppet that you can control to be a perfect daughter with perfect grades. *(Turning towards ABI)* She was struggling, and you didn't even notice. *(Beat)* Evelyn was an amazing friend. I don't know what I would've done without her. In all honesty, I would have been dead a long time ago if it weren't for her support. She talked to me, I talked to her. I know I was a horrible friend at times. That was the biggest mistake I've ever made. Evelyn was kind. She was talented. She gave so much into her life and asked for nothing in return. She confessed to me. She told me all about her life at home. *(Turning towards GAVIN)* Gavin, she loved you. You can't ignore the fact that she loved you. We told each other everything. We were the best of friends. She was the best part of my life for 13 years. We were so close that it was like I could read her thoughts. I could hear the little voice in her head talking to mine. In fact, I feel like I can still hear her now. I can hear her talking to all of us.

EMMA takes a deep breath. EVELYN II stands by EMMA and EMMA II.

Evelyn II, Emma, Emma II: I think you can hear her too. She's telling you to notice something about someone today. Look a little deeper into someone's life. See if there's something in their head that they want to let out. If so, let it out. Let the voice in your head speak up and say how you truly feel. Say no to an unnecessary task. Say yes to an extra kind gesture. Explain to someone what you're thinking, what you need to say.

Emma: Evelyn was a fantastic person. We're here today because of her. She deserved so much more in life. She deserved so much happiness, so many good memories. I-I...

EMMA begins to break down crying.

Emma: I'm so sorry I can't give that to her. If at this very moment I could give her a hug, I would. I would tell her how much she was loved, how much she was appreciated and <u>needed</u> in our lives. Evelyn, if you can hear me now, know that I'm sorry. Know that I love you. Know that <u>we</u> love you. Know that the voice in my head is making sure to tell you that <u>I love you.</u>

Lights Fade Out
A spotlight is kept on EMMA at the microphone. EVELYN II circles around EMMA before giving her a big hug. EMMA is still crying, and doesn't feel the hug, as she does not know EVELYN II is there. No one knows.

Evelyn II: Oh, Emma. I love you too. I wish I could talk to you again. Tell you how much you did mean to me. You stuck by my side for thirteen years and I would do anything to have that time back. You were my rock. I know you can't really hear me, but I hope the little voice in the back of your mind is communicating some of the many things I need to say to you. You are a wonderful person, Emma. You deserve happiness, and it is my fault that I took that away from you. I'm so sorry.

EVELYN II puts her hands on EMMA'S shoulders and gives her a big squeeze. EMMA takes a deep breath and smiles. She knows Evelyn is there with her in that moment and will cherish this final squeeze for a long time.

Spotlight Fades Out

Scene 9

Entire cast except EVELYN stands in a line at the front of the stage. The casket and vases of flowers are still in the background. EVELYN II stands next to ABI in the middle. Next to ABI stands GAVIN and CONNOR. Next to EVELYN II stands EMMA and AVA.

Evelyn II: This concludes the crazy story of the world inside my head. The world inside-

EVELYN II motions to the cast around her.

Evelyn II: Our heads. The world inside-

EVELYN II motions to the audience, breaking the fourth wall.

Evelyn II: Your heads. Mental illnesses are an important thing. They need to be addressed as soon as they start. Life, love, and learning to speak up are also very important. Maybe things would've turned out better,

Abi: If I had been more supportive.

Connor: If I could hear what he had to say.

Ava: If I could see what's beyond her smile.

Gavin: If I could've known her sense of hope.

Emma: If I could've known her struggles.

ALL: If I listened to the voice in my head, the one that should've been let out,

Evelyn II: Maybe, just maybe, things would turn out-

ALL: Different.

All lights dim except for the spotlight on the casket. EVELYN II circles around it before plucking a lily from a bouquet of flowers on a stand. EVELYN II sets the flower down on the casket and steps into the darkness as the light fades to a blackout.

End of Act 2.

End of play.

J.M. Barrie: Write about the talking whale.

Peter Llewelyn-Davies: What talking whale?

J.M. Barrie: The one that's trapped in your imagination and desperate to get out.

- Finding Neverland

Afterword

Well hey there! Thanks for reading my play. It's been a long, inspiring journey. Since I've now shared Emma, Evelyn, and Gavin's stories, I thought I'd give you a glimpse of mine.

In 2015 I was diagnosed with clinical depression and social anxiety. I didn't think too much of it then, as I was just starting middle school and had way more to focus on than mental issues. I was going to therapy each week, but it took me a while to notice that it wasn't helping at all. In 2016, I switched to just medication. I was feeling better for short periods of time, and would have frequent downward spirals. 2017 was a year that hit me like a truck. I couldn't stay in one piece. I felt broken down and worthless. I, sadly, listened to what my own voice in my head was telling me and acted on these emotions, ultimately leading to a stay at a mental hospital. While there, I was inspired to learn about other people's stories and experiences. When I got back home, I knew I needed to shine some light on mental illnesses, but didn't know how. I somehow managed to get through 7th grade, and couldn't wait for a fresh start in 8th. In 8th grade at the school I attended, we had to do a huge community service project. I immediately knew I wanted to do something on mental illnesses. I really enjoy Broadway musicals and plays, so what better way to combine my love for those with my love for writing, than in a play all about mental illnesses? The words for this wonderful story seemed to flow right out of me, as I waited 3 years to say all of this. But, it was also super hard to write. Mental illnesses are a heavy and touchy subject that people don't usually talk about. So, I wrote this in order to shed some light on the real-life struggles people go through every day. I did lots of research on the facts behind mental illnesses and interviewed lots of people to get real stories. It takes lots of courage to share stories like this. Thank you to everyone who helped me with the research that was necessary for this piece of writing. I hope Evelyn's story inspired you to speak up and NOT act on your emotions. I hope Emma's story inspired you to not hide behind a fake smile. I hope Gavin's story inspired you to believe in courage. I hope the voices in your head are good, and inspire you to believe in yourself and others. Let your "love lily" blossom today. Much love and thanks to everyone reading this. Stay safe and speak up.

USA National Crisis Hotline:

1-800-273-8255

(1-800-273-TALK)

About the Author

Kali Mick likes to write; a lot. This is her first published book and is looking to publish more in the future. She currently resides in Colorado but is a California girl at heart. She is a devoted Disney Parks, Star Wars and musical theatre enthusiast with an unmatched sense of humor. Thanks for following along on the first step of her writing journey. Oh, and revive Great Comet. @kali.mick (2020)

Printed in Great Britain
by Amazon

74445642R00041